Donut and P

The Frisbee

by Richard Thomas

Important Info!

The treats given to Donut and Pickles are homemade with ingredients that are safe for them. Before feeding anything to your dog, please consult a veterinarian to be certain it is safe for your particular dog's breed.

Thank You!

“Get up Pickles. Our girl, Felicity, is going to take us to the park,” said Donut.
“I’m only going if you saw her pack pickles.”

“Well, she does have a picnic basket and I bet there are donuts and pickles in it,” said Donut.

“Alright, I’ll go,” agreed Pickles.

When they arrived at the park, they saw their friend Luna.

Her boy, Zack, was throwing a frisbee and
Luna was catching it.

"Luna can really leap!" noticed Pickles.
"Yes she can," Donut agreed.

Time and again Luna ran, leaped, and caught the frisbee in her mouth.

But then, something went wrong.

"Oh no Pickles! Luna's frisbee is in the stream. It's time for me to win Luna's heart and maybe even earn a donut."

He took off running towards the stream as Pickles waddled behind him.

"It's out in the middle. I can't reach it. What should we do Pickles?"
"Don't ask me," answered Pickles. "You're the thinker."

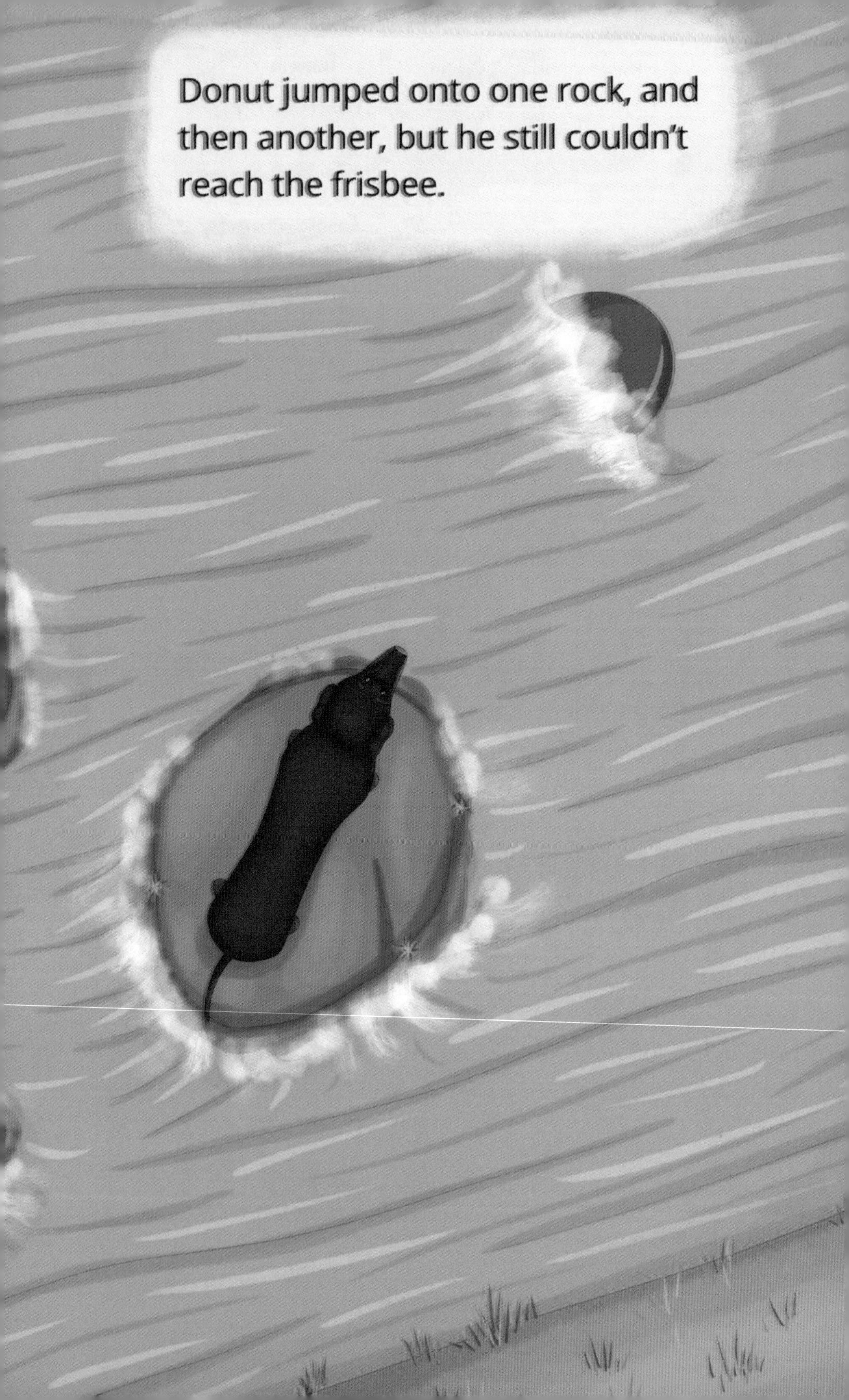
Donut jumped onto one rock, and then another, but he still couldn't reach the frisbee.

"Pickles hold my tail in your mouth as I stretch to reach the frisbee," ordered Donut.
"What? No way. Your tail is dirty," scowled Pickles.

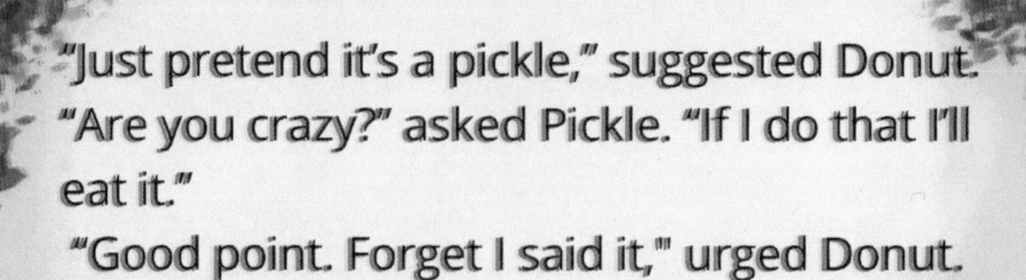

"Just pretend it's a pickle," suggested Donut.
"Are you crazy?" asked Pickle. "If I do that I'll eat it."
"Good point. Forget I said it," urged Donut.

Donut quickly ran downstream
searching for a way to get the frisbee
before it was gone for good.

Donut picked up a large stick in his mouth and desperately tried to stop and pull the frisbee to shore, but it just slipped right by the stick.

Donut knew a lot was riding on this rescue, so he wasn't about to give up. "Get quiet. Center. Let the solution come to you," he said to himself.

"I've got it Pickles. I'm going to jump into the stream from that big rock and snatch the frisbee. Then you lean down from that fallen tree and grab the frisbee in your mouth and pull me out. But don't miss or I'll get washed over the waterfall."

"Ok," agreed Pickles. "The frisbee is a lot cleaner than your tail."

Donut ran up onto and then leaped off the rock. He splashed into the water right next to the frisbee and grabbed it in his mouth. Then, Donut raised it above the water as the stream pulled him toward the waterfall.

Pickles carefully balanced on the fallen tree, bent down, and grabbed the other end of the frisbee in his mouth just in time. He then pulled Donut to the shore ending the Frisbee Fiasco.

Luna smiled with excitement. "You're so brave Donut. Thank you so much for saving my frisbee!" Zack and Felicity were amazed too.

"Look what we have for you brave boys," said Felicity as she pulled out homemade dog friendly pickles and donuts from the picnic basket. The boys wasted no time in eating them.

"That was delicious," said Pickles.
"It sure was," replied Donut. "Now, I wonder how we can earn another treat?"

Thank You For Your Support!

Printed in Great Britain
by Amazon